Willy & Max

A Holocaust Story

Amy
Littlesugar

illustrated by
William Low

PHILOMEL BOOKS

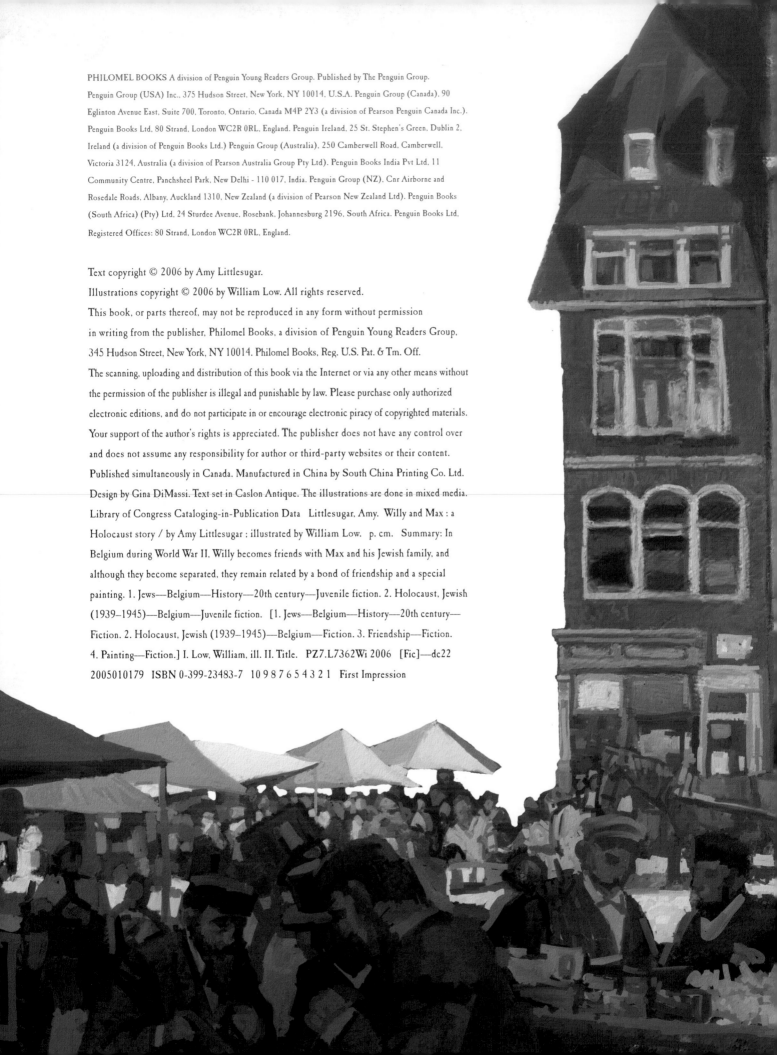

PHILOMEL BOOKS A division of Penguin Young Readers Group. Published by The Penguin Group.
Penguin Group (USA) Inc., 375 Hudson Street, New York, NY 10014, U.S.A. Penguin Group (Canada), 90
Eglinton Avenue East, Suite 700, Toronto, Ontario, Canada M4P 2Y3 (a division of Pearson Penguin Canada Inc.).
Penguin Books Ltd, 80 Strand, London WC2R 0RL, England. Penguin Ireland, 25 St. Stephen's Green, Dublin 2,
Ireland (a division of Penguin Books Ltd.) Penguin Group (Australia), 250 Camberwell Road, Camberwell,
Victoria 3124, Australia (a division of Pearson Australia Group Pty Ltd). Penguin Books India Pvt Ltd, 11
Community Centre, Panchsheel Park, New Delhi - 110 017, India. Penguin Group (NZ), Cnr Airborne and
Rosedale Roads, Albany, Auckland 1310, New Zealand (a division of Pearson New Zealand Ltd). Penguin Books
(South Africa) (Pty) Ltd, 24 Sturdee Avenue, Rosebank, Johannesburg 2196, South Africa. Penguin Books Ltd,
Registered Offices: 80 Strand, London WC2R 0RL, England.

Published simultaneously in Canada. Manufactured in China by South China Printing Co. Ltd.
Design by Gina DiMassi. Text set in Caslon Antique. The illustrations are done in mixed media.
Library of Congress Cataloging-in-Publication Data   Littlesugar, Amy. Willy and Max : a
Holocaust story / by Amy Littlesugar ; illustrated by William Low. p. cm. Summary: In
Belgium during World War II, Willy becomes friends with Max and his Jewish family, and
although they become separated, they remain related by a bond of friendship and a special
painting. 1. Jews—Belgium—History—20th century—Juvenile fiction. 2. Holocaust, Jewish
(1939–1945)—Belgium—Juvenile fiction. [1. Jews—Belgium—History—20th century—
Fiction. 2. Holocaust, Jewish (1939–1945)—Belgium—Fiction. 3. Friendship—Fiction.
4. Painting—Fiction.] I. Low, William, ill. II. Title. PZ7.L7362Wi 2006 [Fic]—dc22
2005010179 ISBN 0-399-23483-7 10 9 8 7 6 5 4 3 2 1 First Impression

Special thanks to Christian and Derek.
—W. L.

Long ago in the city of Antwerp, when my grandpa Will was just a boy, his parents owned an antique shop in a tall, narrow house on Twelve Months Street. It was always filled with unusual things, and you never knew what you might find—a mummy's crown, a pirate's peg leg, a fire-breathing dragon from ancient China!

One day, Willy's papa put a painting in a golden frame in the shop window. It was called *The Lady*, and she was so beautiful that when you smiled at her, she smiled back!

"Some things," Willy's papa would remind him as they gazed upon The Lady's secret smile, "are as precious as friends."

Only Willy, who was very shy, wanted a real friend. Someone he could play with beside the great stone fountain in the park.

Then, one evening, a man and a young boy came
into the shop. The man said his name was Professor
Solomon. He'd seen *The Lady* in the window.

"She smiled at me," he told Willy's papa.

"Then you must have her," said Papa. "Let me wrap
her for you."

Willy, meanwhile, was left alone with the boy.

"What's your name?" the boy asked.

"Willy," said Willy softly. "What's yours?"

"Max," said the boy.

"Where do you live?" Willy asked, feeling braver.

Max put his hands on his hips. "Near the Pelikaanstrasse,"
he said, chin up. "The Jewish quarter."

The Jewish quarter! Suddenly, Willy remembered what Papa'd told him.
How, far away, a war was brewing like a summer storm. How angry
soldiers were marching into the streets where Jewish people lived.
Jewish people like Max.

Willy looked at Max. He had bright blue eyes.
He was missing a front tooth—just like Willy.
"Watch this," said Max, and he began
to whistle.
Willy wished he could whistle that good!
"Do you—do you like to play
hide-and-seek?" he asked, hoping.
"Of course." Max grinned, and Willy
leaped into the air.
"Come on, then!"

Down they went into a cellar as big as a cave. Here Willy's papa kept the biggest antiques—the ones that weighed so much, they needed chains and ropes to move them.

"Wow!" Max's eyes were big with wonder.

But Willy was used to the old pipe organ and the dusty suits of armor.

"You count," he told Max.

"1-2-3-4-5," began Max, and Willy ran quickly to a bronze angel with folded wings—his favorite hiding place. In a secret hollow between its wings, Willy made himself very small.

"I'll find you!" Max's voice echoed.

They took turns running, hiding and laughing—especially when Max tried to fit inside a dusty suit of armor. Willy didn't feel shy with Max, and he was sorry when Professor Solomon came to the top of the cellar steps and said Max had to go home.

"Let's meet at the park," Max suggested. "Tomorrow—by the big stone fountain!"

Willy's eyes were shining. The park! He could hardly wait.

The next day Max was waiting, as he'd promised.

"Look what I brought," he announced. "Soap, sticks. All we need's some paper for the sails and we'll have two boats."

Willy loved to make boats. And newspapers made perfect sails! He poked around in a nearby trash can and found one.

GERMAN TROOPS INVADE NORWAY!

Willy froze. The faraway war wasn't far away anymore! Soon, maybe, the soldiers would be marching into Antwerp—into the Jewish quarter where Max lived. Hastily, Willy tore the page off of the newspaper and threw it away.

"Here, Max," he called. "I've found our sails!"

For the rest of the afternoon, Willy and Max were pirates on the high seas. The sun was soft and warm. And only once did Willy shiver.

The weeks passed quickly. If a war was coming, Willy and Max
never talked of it—and they were never apart.

One time, Max brought a camera to the park. He asked a
policeman to take their picture.

"Now," said Max, his arm around Willy,
"we'll be friends forever."

And Willy knew it must be true, for one Friday night, Max invited him
to *erev Shabbos*—their Sabbath dinner.

Willy loved the way the house smelled of soap and floor wax. The way the
silver candlesticks flickered and glowed.

"You're like family to us, Willy," Professor Solomon said warmly.

After dinner he told the boys the stories of Abraham, Daniel and Esther,
while The Lady, on a carved rosewood easel, smiled nearby.

There was no mention of war.

One afternoon at Willy's house, he and Max sat listening
to the radio. They could hear the sound of a thousand cheering
voices—and one, louder and angrier than the rest.

"The Jews are the enemy of the German people!" it screamed
into Mama's kitchen, and Mama took Max into her arms and
held him close.

But they all knew it was no longer safe.

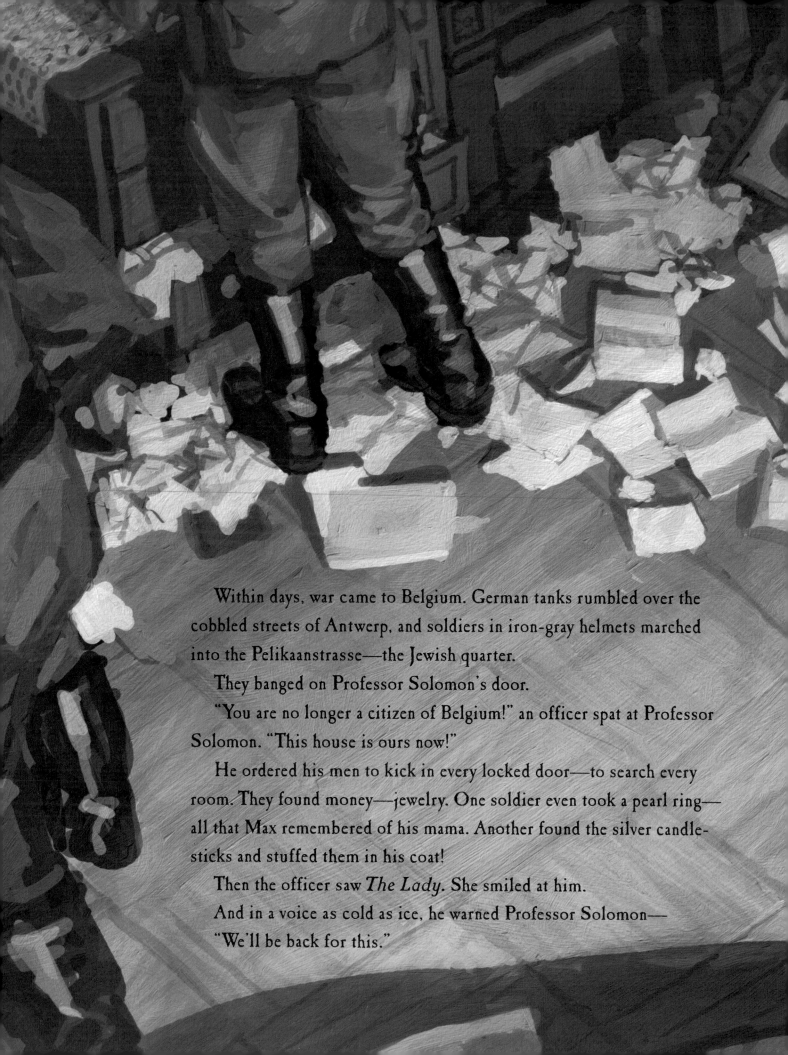

Within days, war came to Belgium. German tanks rumbled over the cobbled streets of Antwerp, and soldiers in iron-gray helmets marched into the Pelikaanstrasse—the Jewish quarter.

They banged on Professor Solomon's door.

"You are no longer a citizen of Belgium!" an officer spat at Professor Solomon. "This house is ours now!"

He ordered his men to kick in every locked door—to search every room. They found money—jewelry. One soldier even took a pearl ring—all that Max remembered of his mama. Another found the silver candlesticks and stuffed them in his coat!

Then the officer saw *The Lady.* She smiled at him.

And in a voice as cold as ice, he warned Professor Solomon—

"We'll be back for this."

The next day, Max told Willy everything that happened.
"Papa says we may have to leave Antwerp," he said sadly.
They sat in the park and Max wore a little yellow star on his coat.
Willy missed him already.

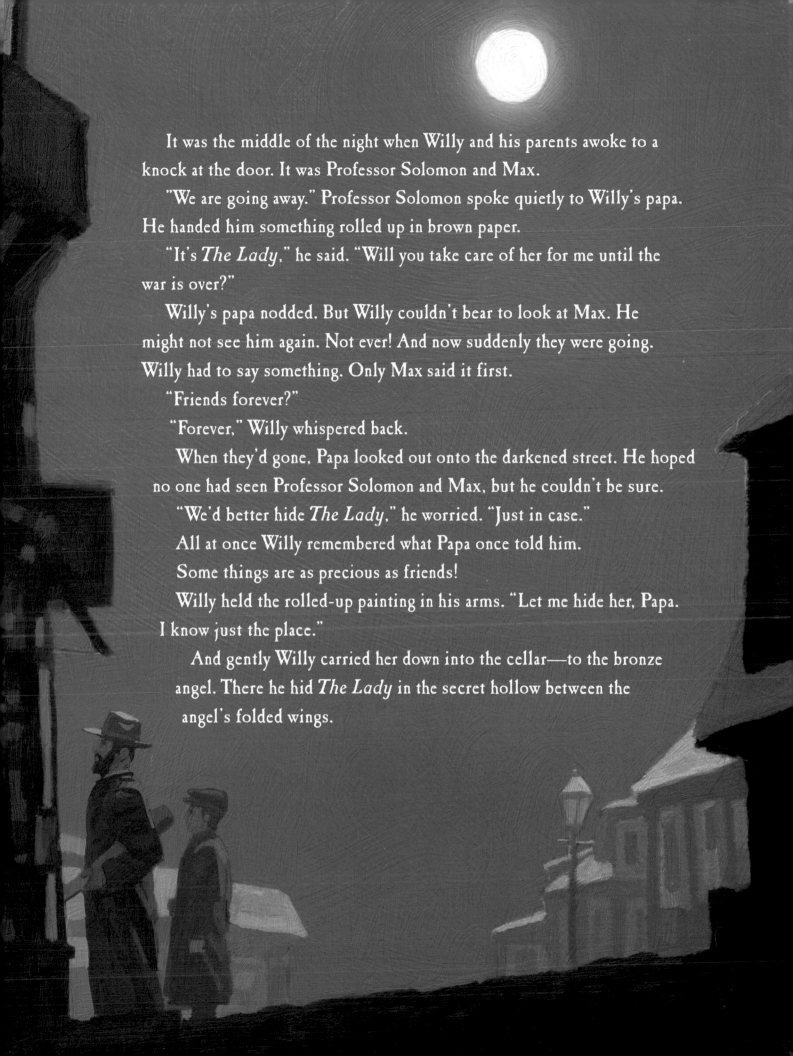

It was the middle of the night when Willy and his parents awoke to a
knock at the door. It was Professor Solomon and Max.

"We are going away." Professor Solomon spoke quietly to Willy's papa.
He handed him something rolled up in brown paper.

"It's *The Lady*," he said. "Will you take care of her for me until the
war is over?"

Willy's papa nodded. But Willy couldn't bear to look at Max. He
might not see him again. Not ever! And now suddenly they were going.
Willy had to say something. Only Max said it first.

"Friends forever?"

"Forever," Willy whispered back.

When they'd gone, Papa looked out onto the darkened street. He hoped
no one had seen Professor Solomon and Max, but he couldn't be sure.

"We'd better hide *The Lady*," he worried. "Just in case."

All at once Willy remembered what Papa once told him.

Some things are as precious as friends!

Willy held the rolled-up painting in his arms. "Let me hide her, Papa.
I know just the place."

And gently Willy carried her down into the cellar—to the bronze
angel. There he hid *The Lady* in the secret hollow between the
angel's folded wings.

A few days later, the soldiers did come. "Open up!" they
shouted, pounding on the door.

A Nazi officer pushed roughly past Papa, glancing at Willy.
Willy shivered. The officer's voice was like ice.

"You've been seen talking to Jews!" he lashed out at Papa.
"Maybe you hide things for them as well?"

Willy squeezed Mama's hand.

"No," Papa lied.

"We'll see," said the soldier sharply.

The soldiers hunted everywhere in Willy's house. Upstairs in his room, in Mama's kitchen. Willy heard drawers squeak open, pots clatter. He saw the soldiers go through every paper on Papa's desk.

"Where does this door go?" demanded the first soldier.

"To the cellar," Papa said carefully.

Down they all went into the cellar as big as a cave. Past the old pipe organ and the dusty suits of armor. Past the bronze angel with the folded wings. Willy's heart was beating fast.

"There's nothing here!" the soldier said impatiently, and Willy could almost breathe.

The Lady was safe!

But as the soldier turned to leave, the bronze angel caught his eye.

"I think I want this," he told Willy's papa.

Willy could see Papa's hands clenched tightly behind his back. But softly he answered, "It's not for sale."

The soldier grinned. "Oh, no? Then I'll just take it."

And Willy watched helplessly as chains and ropes were brought to take away his angel—and *The Lady*, hidden inside.

"Oh, Max!" Willy's heart cried out.

But there was nothing—nothing—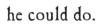
he could do.

More than sixty years passed. Willy grew up and moved to
America. He was my grandpa Will now with many stories to tell.
But the ones about the war he kept to himself—till one day.

A big museum in the city called. They'd found something
they were sure belonged to him. Would he come and see it?

The curator at the museum smiled as Grandpa Will entered her office. "It's over there." She pointed.

But Grandpa Will had already found it—a painting of a beautiful lady!

"She was discovered after the war," the curator said, "in the bombed-out rubble of a German city. It was hidden in the broken wing of an angel."

Then she showed Grandpa Will a yellowed photograph that had been taped to the back of the canvas.

"We tried to find this other boy, but couldn't. We were lucky to find you."

Grandpa Will smiled remembering the two boys, their arms around each other. "Willy and Max," it said. "Friends forever."

Grandpa Will took *The Lady* home that day. We hung it in Grandpa Will's room. But he still wasn't happy. Every night he sat in his rocking chair, thinking.

Finally he asked the curator at the museum to try harder to find Max.

It took a long, long time, but at last she did.

"Max died last year," she told Grandpa Will sadly. "But he has a family living in New Jersey."

So that was where we all went—the whole family—one Friday evening.

A man with bright blue eyes greeted us at the door. He said he was Max's son.

"Come in," the man said happily. "You're like family to us!"

There was a handshake. Then a hug. And tears. Lots of tears!

"This belongs to you," said Grandpa Will. And carefully he handed him the painting of *The Lady*.

The man couldn't stop looking at it. "How often my father spoke of her," he said gently. "And of you, Will."

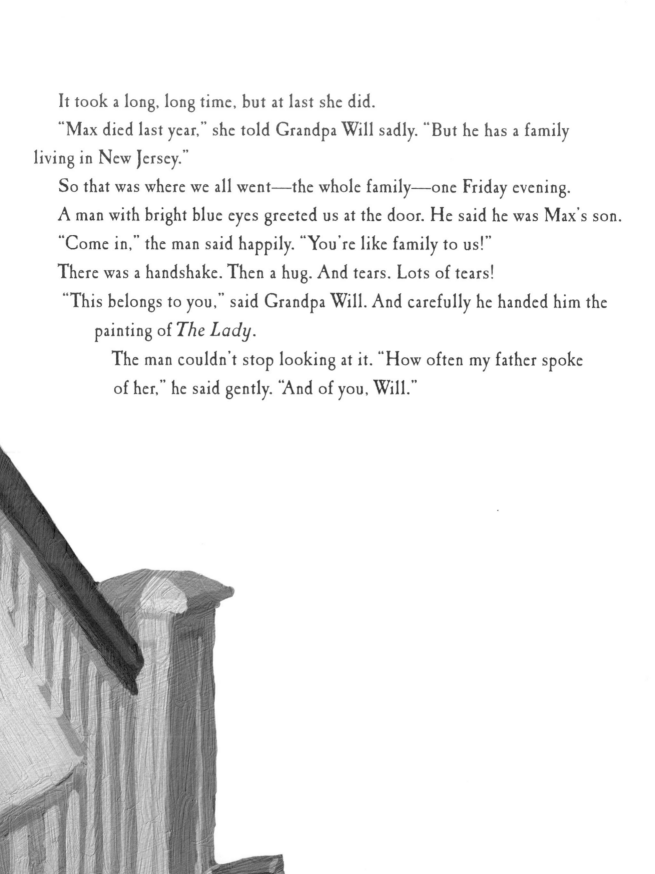

That night we stayed for *erev Shabbos*. Silver candlesticks
flickered and glowed, and wine was poured. Even for me. Then
Grandpa Will made a toast. He smiled at The Lady. She smiled back.
"To some things," he said softly, "as precious as friends."
And he looked across the table at Max's family.
"Well, almost."

AUTHOR'S NOTE

"Finders, keepers"—that's what some people think when they find something that doesn't belong to them. That alone is wrong. But during the grim years of World War II, the Nazis weren't only finders—they found and stole hundreds of thousands of artworks from all over Europe. Many of these treasures belonged to Jewish people—the greatest victims of Nazi hatred.

After the war, much of this stolen artwork was recovered, and if it could be traced back to the real owners, the way The Lady was returned to Max's family, it was. But in most cases there were no photographs on the backs of paintings or sculptures—no letters telling museums whom the artwork once belonged to. Instead, wealthy art buyers and auction houses kept the artwork—even when they knew the painful history attached to most of them—even when they knew that stamped somewhere on a frame might be the crooked black cross of the Nazis.

Today, museum task forces like The Commission for Art Recovery are working hard to reunite stolen Jewish artworks with their rightful owners. Maybe now, family heirlooms like The Lady can be more than a memory.